CLUELESS McGEE
Gets Famous!

Jeff Mack

PHILOMEL BOOKS
An Imprint of Penguin Group (USA)

ALSO BY JEFF MACK:
CLUELESS MCGEE
CLUELESS MCGEE AND THE INFLATABLE PANTS

PHILOMEL BOOKS
Published by the Penguin Group
Penguin Group (USA) LLC, 375 Hudson Street, New York, NY 10014

USA | Canada | UK | Ireland | Australia | New Zealand | India | South Africa | China
penguin.com A Penguin Random House Company

Library of Congress Cataloging-in-Publication Data
Mack, Jeff. Clueless McGee gets famous / Jeff Mack. pages cm.—(Clueless McGee ; 3) Summary: When Clueless learns that the scribble on the cowboy hat sent by his father is actually the autograph of teen idol Junior McFiddle, everyone in school suddenly wants to be Clueless's friend—and they want his hat. [1. Behavior—Fiction. 2. Schools—Fiction. 3. Private investigators—Fiction. 4. Autographs—Fiction. 5. Robbers and outlaws—Fiction. 6. Popularity—Fiction. 7. Humorous stories.] I. Title. PZ7.M18973Cng 2014 [Fic]—dc23 2013021285
Printed in the United States of America. ISBN 978-0-399-25751-3
1 3 5 7 9 10 8 6 4 2
Edited by Michael Green. Design by Semadar Megged.

The illustrations are rendered in pencil on paper.

For Emily,
an awesome sister.
And a seriously epic mom!

Chapter One

The Famous Letter

Dear Dad,

You'll never believe it, but I saw a world-famous hero go to the nurse's office today.

And it wasn't even my fault! I swear!

It all started during silent reading, when Mrs. Sikes made a special announcement.

Officer Bill is this local policeman who visits schools and teaches kids how to be safe. He thinks he's really cool and funny, but I'm not even sure he's a real cop. He visits so many schools, he doesn't actually have time to save lives or catch any bad guys. Plus, real cops aren't supposed to rhyme.

As you know, safety is pretty much the most boring subject ever. So Officer Bill tries to add something "new" and "exciting" to his show every year. Usually it's dancing. For instance, when I was in third grade, he was Officer Bill, the tap-dancing policeman.

And the year after that, he was Officer Bill, the belly-dancing policeman.

I never thought he'd get invited back after that.

Trust me, Dad. I would have been happy if this year's famous guest was anyone but Officer Bill.

When we got to the cafeteria, Mr. Prince was already on the stage with his megaphone.

Pretty much no one clapped as Officer Bill walked out from behind the flag. Then, instead of break-dancing, he started talking to a horse puppet! It looked like it was going to be another terrible show.

No one laughed. Not only were the horse's jokes horrible, he looked totally fake. You could even see his lips moving. Officer Bill's lips, I mean. Not the horse's.

Officer Bill said he was going to teach us what to do if one of our friends (or horses) ever choked on a carrot. But first, he needed a volunteer.

No one raised their hand. So finally, Mr. Prince stepped forward.

The crowd cheered as our band teacher went onstage. He put his hand up to his neck and pretended to gag while Officer Bill ran around behind him.

Mr. Pastrami didn't budge.

He just stood there, sweating as usual.

Officer Bill shut his eyes and squeezed harder.
His face turned beet red. His feet started sliding
in Mr. Pastrami's sweat drops on the floor.

ARE YOU SQUEEZING YET?

It was useless. Finally, Officer Bill sat down
and wiped his face with Mr. Prince's handkerchief.

No one cheered.

OK, BOYS AND GIRLS! LET'S HEAR IT FOR OFFICER BILL!

CAN I STOP CHOKING NOW?

I DON'T CARE.

Mr. Toots walked onto the stage and started mopping the floor. I thought it was all over for Officer Bill.

He stood back up.

Someone made a rude noise. I'll bet it was Jack B., because he got sent to the office. That didn't stop Officer Bill, though.

He squatted down and stuck out one leg.

THIS MOVE IS CALLED THE SAFETY GRINDER!

Then he started to spin. His leg went around and around. Soon he was going really fast!

OH, YEAH!

For a second, I thought he was going to slip in Mr. Toots's puddle.

DON'T TOUCH THAT!

But he didn't.

He kicked the flagpole instead.

CLANG!

DON'T TOUCH **THAT!**

WOO-HOO!

The flagpole tipped backward into the curtain. Then the whole curtain came crashing down!

It landed right on top of Officer Bill!

Then Mr. Toots's bucket fell on his head.

Everyone burst into applause. Let me tell you, Dad—I've heard kids cheer before, but never like this. It was incredible!

As it turns out, Officer Bill isn't just about safety. He's also about doing some of the most dangerous break-dancing moves I've ever seen. If you ask me, he's a true hero! He might even be a ninja!

I only wish I got his autograph before he went to the nurse.

When I got home, I tried to show Mom and Chloe how to do the Safety Grinder, Officer Bill style! But they were too busy watching a video by country music star Junior McFiddle on the Internet.

His latest hit single is called "Love Pony." Have you heard it yet? Well, don't bother, because it stinks! It's just Junior with a guitar, going

That's the whole song. Can you believe it? Talk about lame! It doesn't even have any drums in it!

Honestly, Dad. I just don't see what Mom and Chloe like so much about his music.

Mom said listening to "Love Pony" with Chloe is how they spend "quality time" together. But if you ask me, Mom is really going to regret it.

Speaking of quality time, I just had an awesome idea: Remember how you said the Secret Mission has been secretly recording bad guys in Nashville? Well, how about if I come out there and live with you and the other private eyes in your hotel?

That way, I can do some spying too. Plus, I'll
never have to listen to Junior McFiddle again!

I think I'd be a huge help to the Secret Mission.
Not only am I an amazing private eye, I'm also
famous! Remember when I saved Mr. Prince's life
and got my picture taken with all of those firemen?
Well, they printed it in the newspaper! Check it out!

I'm even wearing the awesome cowboy hat you sent me. As you can see, it's pretty much the coolest thing I own.

The only problem is Chloe keeps trying to steal it from me. I think she's jealous. Luckily, I can see right through all her tricks.

Now that I'm famous, I think it's safe to say I'm going to be signing **A LOT** of autographs. So tonight, I borrowed Mom's permanent marker and spent about fifty hours practicing my signature.

As you know, the bigger and messier an autograph is, the more money it's worth. So don't ask me why Mom got so mad. Thanks to all my signatures, now everything in our house is worth a bazillion dollars.

After that, Mom said I wasn't allowed to wear my hat to school tomorrow. She also said I can't borrow her permanent marker anymore.

By the way, did you know that Chloe has been taking ballet lessons? She has a recital this Sunday at the Bunn Community Theater. That means Mom spends pretty much all her time working on the costume. Meanwhile, she totally ignores me. Don't get me wrong. That can be a good thing.

But sometimes it's not.

Since Mom wasn't paying attention right then, I decided to take my hat back. But it was gone!

I had a feeling I knew who took it.

I put on my ninja suit and snuck into Chloe's room.

Sure enough, there it was! Right under the huge poster of Junior McFiddle that you sent her.

There was just one problem: The star was missing!

Not only that, there was a huge messy scribble on the back. I couldn't believe it!

I searched around for clues. And guess what I found?

Her poster had the exact same messy scribble on it!

I think it's safe to say whoever scribbled on the poster also scribbled on my hat!

I sprang into action.

All I can say is, it's a good thing I'm such an awesome private eye. If I hadn't captured her then, who knows what else she would have ruined with her scribbles?

Love,

PJ

PS. Chloe didn't steal my star. Mom did! After I put Chloe in the hamper, Mom walked in with her ballet costume. The star was pinned to the front!

Once I saw that, it didn't take me long to force Mom to confess.

I decided to arrest her too.

As you know, I'm not that easy to deal with.

Chloe still says she didn't scribble on my hat. She swears that both scribbles were there to begin with. But I doubt it. With my incredible eye for detail, I'm pretty sure I would have noticed that.

Chapter Two

The Hat Letter

TUESDAY, MAY 7

Dear Dad,

Today, Mom wouldn't make my breakfast for me.
She said she had to help Chloe pick out a clean
shirt for school. Seriously, Dad. Can't Chloe do
anything for herself?

Meanwhile, I had to put my own jelly on my own bagel. It was ridiculous!

After that, I tried to erase the scribble off my hat. But I couldn't. It was in permanent marker! Mom said no one would notice a little scribble, but let's face it: kids notice everything.

Luckily, I came up with a brilliant plan to hide the scribble using my official Ninja Warz T-shirt.

In fact, I think my hat looked even cooler with the shirt on it!

When I got to school, I expected to see a huge line of kids begging for my autograph.

Actually, there was only one kid.

But you could tell he really wanted it.

Since Dante's only in third grade, I decided to give him a child's discount.

I was about to say forget it, but Dante's also sort of my friend. So I offered him a secret "friendship" deal.

I thought it over. Lucky for him, I was feeling extra generous today.

It turned out the only thing Dante could actually pay me was a piece of gum!

I ended up signing his gum wrapper. It may have been extra small, but it was still worth a fortune.

I seriously have to wonder about the kids in this school, Dad. If you ask me, it would be a lot better if they were all as cool as me. But they're not.

For example, there are these three girls in my grade named Taylor:

TAYLOR E.   TAYLOR P.   TAYLOR Z.

They think they're so cool just because they wear the same Junior McFiddle shirts and listen to the same Junior McFiddle song and talk about Junior McFiddle all day.

They even have their own club called the Taylor Girls. Basically all it means is they wear the same red string bracelets and make fun of everyone who's different from them. If only they could see that I'm the one who's cool. Not them.

I really didn't want to take the shirt off my hat. But the jelly on the bagel was attracting so many flies, I didn't know what else to do.

So I took the shirt off.

Luckily, Dante took a closer look.

Dante said he saw Junior McFiddle wear the exact same hat during his video for "Love Pony." Not only did I have his REAL hat, but I also had his REAL autograph! It was awesome!

Suddenly, everyone started saying how cool my hat was. And how cool I was for wearing it.

Even the Taylor Girls started acting nice to me.

Fame is a funny thing, Dad. One minute everyone is laughing at you, and the next minute you're their hero. All because of a little scribble.

So, Dad, I just have one question for you: How did YOU get Junior McFiddle's hat? And why did he autograph it? Did you meet him in a Nashville hotel? Did the Secret Mission save his life?

Only one thing's for sure: This hat must be worth a bazillion dollars! I had to protect it at all costs!

Me and Mrs. Sikes discussed the best place to put my hat. Finally, after about two hours, she just sent me to the office.

When I got there, Mr. Prince was in a meeting, so I looked around his office for a safe place to hide my hat. I checked his desk, but it was already full.

That's when I found something strange. It was a note on pink paper made out of tiny cut-up letters:

Nasty Ned? Who was that? And why was he telling Mr. Prince to watch it? Was he a bad guy? Was Mr. Prince in danger? Maybe his office wasn't the safest place for my hat after all.

Suddenly, the door creaked open. Was it Nasty
Ned? I dropped the note and sprang into action.

Luckily, it was only Mr. Prince. I think he was
happy to see me too.

As you know, Mr. Prince likes to act tough. But I could tell he was nervous about the note!

I studied him closely. There was a Band-Aid on his forehead. Possibly from a battle.

35

It looked like my work there was finished.

At least for now.

I put my hat on and ran out the door.

I was late for gym.

Believe it or not, I kind of like gym. Coach Hugh is pretty much the best teacher in the school. Probably because he doesn't actually teach anything. He mostly just spends the entire class telling us jokes.

COACH HUGH →

HEY, YOU GUYS! WHAT DO CLOUDS WEAR UNDER THEIR PANTS?

GIVE UP?

UNDERWEAR!

HUH?

I DON'T GET IT.

NO, WAIT. THAT'S NOT RIGHT.

I MEAN THUNDER-WEAR!

GET IT? THUNDERWEAR?

He's totally hilarious!

HA! HA! HA! HA! THUNDERWEAR!

When he's not coaching gym class, Coach Hugh directs all our school plays. I've heard he even writes some of them himself.

Dante told me Coach Hugh once tried to be a stand-up comic. But for some reason, he never got famous. So he became a gym teacher. Luckily, this job is perfect for him. Not only is he really funny and cool, he knows every sports joke ever written.

When I got to gym today, there was a sign on the door.

Ever since Officer Bill's visit yesterday, I've dreamed of being a professional break-dancer.

Break-dancing is pretty much doing ninja moves to music, so you could tell I was definitely going to be awesome at it. There was only one problem:

As if that wasn't bad enough, we had to dance with a partner! I looked around to see who I should pick. It was a tough choice.

Luckily, Coach Hugh said he was going to make it easy for us.

It turned out, the list didn't exactly make things any easier.

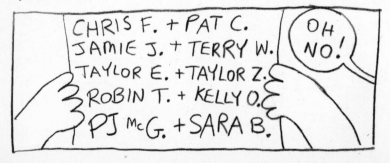

Let's face it. There are some kids here who no one wants to be partners with.

Coach Hugh told everyone to start out by holding their partner's hand. As you know, there's nothing worse than having to hold hands with a girl. Especially when it's Sara. Talk about humiliating!

Then, before I could stop him, Coach Hugh took my hat!

MIND IF I BORROW THIS, BIG GUY?

JmF

HEY!

He put it on his own head!

LOOK, YOU GUYS! I'M A COWBOY!!

I was pretty sure things couldn't get any worse.

Then he started the music.

PONY! PONY! PONY! PONY! PONY! PONY! LOVE!

I HOPE YOU GUYS LIKE JUNIOR McFIDDLE!

As soon as they heard "Love Pony," everyone got really excited and started dancing however they wanted. Some used hula hoops. Some used dodge balls.

Meanwhile, Coach Hugh tried to teach us a few moves, but no one paid any attention.

Then, Mr. Pastrami walked in!

Somehow, a dodge ball got jammed inside his tuba.

Mr. Pastrami blew hard. The tuba made this weird blarpy sound:

And the ball popped back out.

It flew across the room toward Coach Hugh and knocked my hat right off his head.

After that, the entire room went crazy! Dodge balls started flying everywhere! So did my hat!

I saw someone kick it across the room. Then it disappeared into the crowd.

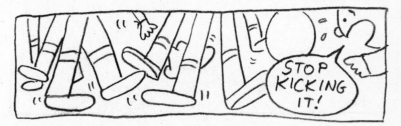

Finally, Coach Hugh blew his whistle, and everyone froze. Everyone but me, that is!

Coach Hugh said that my hat was probably just missing.

LET'S ASK MR. PASTRAMI IF HE'S SEEN IT.

But Mr. Pastrami was missing too!

" "

HAS ANYONE HERE SEEN MR. PASTRAMI?

I THINK HIS TUBA BROKE.

"

As usual, I stayed calm. But it wasn't easy.

STOLEN! MY HAT WAS STOLEN!

Coach Hugh put his hand on my shoulder.

To be honest, I didn't think that was very funny.

As soon as I got home, I told Mom what happened.
But she was too busy to care.

As usual, Chloe was no help either.

What am I going to do, Dad? That hat was the only reason people liked me! If I don't get it back, I'll never be famous again!

I think I might need your help with this.

Love,
PJ

48

PS. Never mind! I don't need help. I figured out how I'm going to catch the hat thief:

First, I'll chop him with an awesome slide kick.

Then I'll turn it into a triumphant Safety Grinder!

That way, I can become a famous crime fighter and a famous break-dancer all at the same time! Pretty amazing, huh?

Not only that, my ninja suit is perfect for doing both kinds of moves! On a smooth floor, I can slide at least a hundred feet without even stopping!

As you can see, the hat thief doesn't stand a chance against moves like mine.

Chapter Three

The Breakin' Letter

Dear Dad,

It turns out being a break-dancer is way easier than I thought. Check out these incredible moves I invented:

Not only are they all totally original, they're even more dangerous than Officer Bill's moves!

Even Mom was impressed. After about an hour, she told me I was all done practicing. I guess she can tell that I'm already an expert.

So here's my new plan: You invite me to Nashville, and I'll teach all of the private eyes in the Secret Mission my greatest break-dancing hits. For free! Then you can use my moves whenever you want to defeat bad guys. What do you say? Is it a deal?

Please say yes. I've got to get out of here soon. This song is driving me crazy!

Speaking of songs, on the bus this morning I wrote my own hit single. And it's about something way cooler than love or ponies. You guessed it: break-dancing!

By the time I got to school, I knew I had written a masterpiece! Seriously, Dad. It was so good, I just had to sing it out loud during silent reading.

Well, what do you think, Dad? I can't tell which is more awesome, my moves or my song about my moves. Even Mrs. Sikes was amazed. At first, she just stood there shaking with excitement. Then, she told me to go to the office.

When I got to his office, Mr. Prince was laughing at a bunch of pink papers he was reading. You could tell he has amazing respect for my moves, because when he saw me, he stopped laughing.

I started singing my hit single right there in front of his desk.

I would have done the whole thing, but Mr. Prince said I should save my moves for the after-school dance party next Thursday.

I was stunned! A dance party? How come I had
never heard of that before?

Mr. Prince handed me a stack of papers.

I said I'd make sure everyone saw the posters.
After all, this was my big chance to show the
whole school my famous moves!

No trophies?! On second thought, I didn't need a dance party to show off my moves. I could break-dance anytime I wanted to.

So I decided to hang the posters up.

Suddenly, the door opened, and I slammed right into Coach Hugh. He was carrying a big stack of pink papers, and they all went flying.

So did the posters.

Luckily, Coach Hugh didn't seem too mad about it. In fact, he even helped me pick a few of them up.

When I got to lunch, Mrs. Browny was serving one of my all-time favorite foods: cheesy sweet dogs!

YUM-YUM!

These are regular hot dogs dipped in a sweet cheesy sauce. As usual, I got two.

Unfortunately, the cheese dripped all over the posters and made them really sticky.

WHY DO YOU HAVE SO MANY PAPERS, PJ?

THEY'RE NOT PAPERS, DANTE. THEY'RE POSTERS.

OH.

CAN I SEE?

SURE, CATCH!

One of them stuck to Dante.

Believe it or not, he was right. It was a note from Nasty Ned!

As usual, Dante looked confused.

Everyone knows a "ten gallon" is what a cowboy calls his hat! Nasty Ned was talking about my autographed Junior McFiddle hat! This note was proof that he stole it! Now the only question was how!

As you can see, the only thing missing was my hat! And there was just one way to find it.

All we had to do was hang wanted posters of Nasty Ned on every single wall in the school. Then someone would see his picture and turn him in. I would get my hat back and become famous at the same time.

It was the perfect plan.

Pretty soon, Sara came over to see what we were working on.

I showed her our awesome new wanted posters.

Sara said if I really wanted to solve the mystery, I should hire her.

Can you believe it? Sara? A private eye? Don't make me laugh! Everyone knows, if you want to be a private eye, you have to master certain skills.

Sara said she's a way better private eye than I'll ever be. But that's impossible. Thanks to my incredible eye for detail, I'm the best private eye in the entire school. No one else even comes close.

Sara really bugs me. She thinks she knows everything, but she really doesn't.

That made no sense at all! Why would it say "ten gallons"?

A real private eye would have known that. See what I mean? When it comes to solving mysteries, Sara is totally clueless.

Love,
PJ

PS. I forgot to tell you. We had art class today. Until now, I always thought art was pretty much useless. I mean, let's face it: No one ever solved a crime or karate-chopped a bad guy with art.

I think a lot of kids just like it because it's the only class where copying isn't considered cheating.

Today, Ms. Julian taught us how to use a grid to copy a picture.

At first, I didn't see the point of copying anything by hand.

Even with the grid, most kids still did a horrible job:

BEFORE   AFTER

BEFORE   AFTER

But thanks to my incredible eye for detail, mine
came out perfect.

BEFORE   AFTER

Even Ms. Julian said so.

Just so you know, Ms. Julian is now my favorite
teacher in the whole school. Even if the stuff she
teaches is mostly useless.

When I got home, Mom was busy as usual. But this time, I didn't mind.

At first I thought it might be a box of ninja throwing stars! Or at least a pair of nunchucks!

It wasn't terrible. But it wasn't as cool as the one you gave me, Dad. So I told her to take it back.

First of all, the REAL hat was a present from you.

And second, this one wasn't even autographed.

Mom said having the signature of a country music star wasn't the most important part of a hat, but she's wrong. The signature is what made me famous!

Then, suddenly, I had a brilliant idea! What if I COULD get famous with a fake hat after all?

While Mom was helping Chloe practice ballet, I snuck into Chloe's room. Then I used my new art skills to copy Junior McFiddle's signature off of Chloe's poster and onto my new fake hat.

Check it out!

Now everyone will think this is the real hat, and I can use it to catch Nasty Ned. Here's my plan:

As you can see, it's perfect! I get my hat back . . .

. . . and no one gets hurt!

Chapter Four

The Muted Tuba Letter

Dear Dad,

This morning, Chloe had a sore throat. Mom said she lost her voice, but you could tell she was just pretending so she could stay home and eat ice pops all day.

As soon as I got to school, I showed Dante my fake hat. I was so excited about it, I just had to do the Ninja Worm. I know I'm not supposed to break-dance during school, but I couldn't help it.

Unfortunately, Ms. Julian saw me.

Luckily, I wasn't actually in trouble.

It's true I'm an awesome artist. But I'm an even awesomer private eye. Plus, I had a crime to solve. So, in the end, I told Ms. Julian I was too busy to waste my time doing something silly like art.

Meanwhile, the Taylor Girls were waiting for me outside the gym. For once, I was almost glad to see them.

I have to admit, it felt good to autograph something. It looked like my new hat had made me famous again. Then I saw what I had just signed.

I had been tricked! I tried to erase my autograph, but it was in permanent marker!

Relax? How could I relax? McFiddle Day was the worst idea I'd ever heard in my life. And I just voted for it! There was nothing I could do except hope they didn't trick anyone else into signing it too.

Luckily, it was time for Ninja Club with Mr. Prince. Me and Dante are the only ones in the club, so the odds are really unfair. As you can see, Mr. Prince doesn't stand a chance against both of us!

Today, Mr. Prince tried to teach us about timing.

He had barely finished his sentence when I sprang into action with about twenty roundhouse kicks to the face. As usual, my timing was perfect!

Not only that, I think one of my kicks might have actually touched him, because the next thing I knew, Mr. Prince's mustache went flying across the room!

Mr. Prince covered his naked lip. I was amazed! Ever since I started break-dancing, my ninja moves have gotten more powerfuller than ever!

Mr. Prince spent the rest of Ninja Club looking for his missing mustache.

By the time Ninja Club was over, the Taylor Girls had left. I figured it was because they couldn't trick enough people into signing their ridiculous McFiddle Day paper.

Meanwhile, Coach Hugh was handing out posters for some kind of playwriting contest.

Coach Hugh said the winner would get to have their play performed in front of the entire school.

Coach Hugh may be a cool guy, but there was no way I was going to sign up to write a play about Junior McFiddle! Especially for something as useless as extra credit!

That's when we saw Sara.

Sara may be kind of smart, but there was no way she could write a whole play by herself. I figured she would give up after an hour. But she didn't. By lunchtime, she seemed more excited than ever.

I figured I would be the last person Sara would ask to be in her play.

To tell you the truth, I almost felt bad for her. But I had way more important things to do than practice lines for her boring play.

As you know, being a private eye is a full-time job. And there was nothing she could say to make me change my mind.

Then again, any play that made me famous couldn't be all bad. So I told her I'd do it.

Trust me, Dad. No one has ever gotten famous being in a play about a love song.

Let's face it: Nothing was ever going to make me join a play called "Love Pony."

If being in Sara's play could stop the Taylor Girls from getting more famous than me, then I was ready to act!

Sara said I won't regret it. I just hope she's right.

Meanwhile, I was late for band. As you know, I've wanted to play the drums for a bazillion years now. Since Mr. Pastrami only lets the most helpful kids play them, I try to get there first and show him how helpful I am. Unfortunately, so does Taylor P.

Today, Coach Hugh got there before both of us. Don't ask me why. Maybe he wants to play the drums too.

While he talked to Mr. Pastrami, I decided to test out my four-step plan to see if anyone in the band was really Nasty Ned in disguise. I skipped right to step three!

Too bad Coach Hugh ruined it before I even got to step four.

I don't get it, Dad. Why does everyone around here have to be so helpful?

I put my hat back on and started cleaning my cymbals with Coach Hugh's towel. Taylor P. tried dusting her xylophone mallets, but you could tell I was being way more helpful than her.

Finally, it was my chance to show everyone my amazing drumming skills! I always knew I'd become a famous drummer someday. Unless, of course, I became a famous private eye, or a famous ninja, or a famous break-dancer, or a famous artist, or a famous actor first.

I sat down at the drum kit. With my fake hat on, I couldn't see a thing. But I could hear everything!

You should have heard me, Dad! I was incredible! I must have smashed every drum and cymbal at least a bazillion times. The whole class was just staring at me. I was a maniac! A rock-and-roll animal!

In the end, I only broke one snare drum, three tom-toms, a high hat, and the bass drum. Other than that, there was no damage at all!

Afterward, Mr. Pastrami asked to borrow my fake hat. He said I'd be a better drummer if I could actually see the drums I was hitting. But I doubt it. How could I ever be better than I am now?

Then he made an announcement.

I never knew Coach Hugh could write songs too. As you can see, he's almost as talented as me!

Mr. Pastrami started to play while Coach Hugh moved my hat around inside his tuba. It made the same blarpy sound that it did during gym class.

Thanks to my hat, his solo didn't sound terrible. But it was so long and boring, everyone fell asleep.

Since Coach Hugh was busy snoring, Mr. Pastrami let Taylor P. take over.

YOU ARE SO HELPFUL, TAYLOR!

GEE, THANKS.

It was no fair, but I was too sleepy to complain. The next thing I knew, I was dreaming that I was sleeping under a cool waterfall. It seemed so real, I could feel drops of water on my face.

Except it wasn't really water.

WAKE UP, PJ!

It was Mr. Pastrami's sweat!

I looked around me. I was the last one in the room. Everyone was gone. Even Coach Hugh.

I checked the tuba, but it wasn't there! It had been stolen, just like the real one! Was this the work of Nasty Ned? Did he sneak into the band room while everyone was asleep?

I couldn't stand it anymore!

Mr. Pastrami said if I was so sure it was stolen, I should report it to Mr. Prince. But he was no help either.

As you can see, my copy was so amazing, even Mr. Prince couldn't tell the difference.

Mr. Prince said it was rude to wear a ten-gallon hat during school. Plus, it was a safety hazard.

That's when I slammed into Coach Hugh. Again! This time, we crashed so hard, his hair literally flew off his head.

I couldn't believe it. Not only did I kick Mr. Prince's mustache off today, I slammed all of Coach Hugh's hair off too! As you can see, my ninja powers have become too powerful for their own good!

He tried to put his hair back on, but as you know, once your hair falls off the first time, it never really fits the same way again. Luckily, he wasn't hurt. Coach Hugh may have lost his hair, but he'll never lose his incredible sense of humor.

Love,
PJ

PS. I didn't really feel like going to Art Club today. Especially after two of my priceless hats were stolen. But since Nasty Ned is on the loose, someone had to be there to protect Ms. Julian.

As it turned out, Taylor E. was the only other kid in Art Club. She may be a nasty kid, but she definitely wasn't Nasty Ned.

Taylor E. was making papier-mâché decorations for the dance party next Thursday. In case you don't know, papier-mâché is where you stick a bunch of wet flour and ripped-up newspapers onto stuff. Then, when it dries, you paint it.

You can pretty much make whatever you want, as long as you cover something that has the same shape as what you're trying to make. For example:

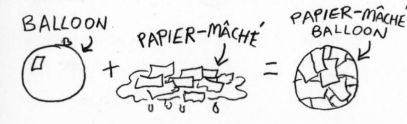

See? It's easy. Plus, it's art!

There was only one problem. All of Taylor E.'s papier-mâché decorations were horrible! Every single thing she made was about Junior McFiddle!

I tried to tell Taylor E. how terrible her decorations looked, but of course she wouldn't listen. So I told Ms. Julian. As an art teacher, I figured she would recognize bad art when she saw it.

But I was wrong. Not only did she like it, she even took pictures.

Ms. Julian said it wasn't my job to tell Taylor E. what she should or shouldn't make.

She said Taylor was free to make whatever she wanted.

Now that I think about it, she had a point. Ninjas are definitely not stupid.

Plus, it gave me an amazing idea for my own decoration.

It's going to take a ton of wet flour and ripped-up newspaper to build it. But once I'm done, it will be more than just an incredible dance party decoration. It will be the ultimate secret weapon!

Ms. Julian tried to take a picture of it, but I stopped her just in time.

Chapter Five

The Audition Letter

Dear Dad,

Did you hear the news? Junior McFiddle started a new band. I don't know what they're called, but everyone at school was talking about their latest hit single, "Bad Guys." I haven't heard it yet, but I'll bet it's even worse than "Love Pony."

Today was the audition for Coach Hugh's playwriting contest. When I got to the cafeteria, Sara was on the stage. So were the Taylor Girls.

Sara looked so nervous, Coach Hugh told the Taylor Girls to go first.

Suddenly they froze.

As it turned out, none of them wrote it! Without a play, they were automatically disqualified! It was awesome!

With the Taylor Girls gone, we were guaranteed to win. But for some reason, Sara still looked nervous.

I opened to the first page.

It was totally blank!

She hadn't written a single line!

I walked out onstage. Before I could even think,
Coach Hugh started yelling directions at me.

I was trapped! I had to act fast!

There was only one thing I could say:

Of course, I was only pretending to lose my voice. But Coach Hugh totally believed me. I guess that's because I'm such an amazing actor!

Thanks to me, Coach Hugh never found out that we didn't actually have a play. He said we could try reading the play again after I got my voice back.

It was only my first performance, but I can already tell I'm going to like being an actor.

Later, me and Sara had a serious talk about the play.

I told Sara that writing was the easiest job in the world. All she had to do was make stuff up and write it down.

As you know, one of my best skills is making stuff up. I can make up stuff about anything: Ninjas. Private eyes. Break-dancing moves. Anything!

Later, on the way to lunch, me and Sara passed the art room.

We went in. The only person there was Taylor P.
She was working on a papier-mâché decoration.
And it looked very familiar.

Taylor E. made the exact same hat yesterday!
Seriously, Dad! How lame can you get?

My project, on the other hand, was totally original.

It was still just a bunch of newspapers and tape. But that's only because I hadn't covered it with papier-mâché yet.

Taylor P. said someone should put it back in the trash where it belonged. Can you believe it? If there's one person who knows nothing about art, it's the Taylor Girls.

I had to hide my art project before any of them tried to copy me.

Luckily, Ms. Julian left a sheet lying nearby.

It was covering a bunch of brightly painted boxes.

As you can see, I had more important things to do than stand around and look at a bunch of boxes.

It turned out they weren't really ice cream. They were just papier-mâché.

As you can see, Sara can be a little bossy. So I was kind of glad she was there to back me up.

Taylor P. said if we didn't leave, she would lie and tell the whole school that I liked Sara.

When we got to lunch, Mrs. Browny was serving two-day-old sweet dogs. Everyone was excited.

I took two and put one in my backpack for later. That's when Dante showed up waving a pink piece of paper. He looked like he'd just seen a ghost.

It was a poster with a picture of Nasty Ned on it! And he was wearing a ten-gallon hat!

Now we knew what he really looked like! There was something strangely familiar about his face.

Nasty Ned was hiding somewhere in the school. I could feel it.

Dante wanted to help, but as you know, part of being a professional break-dancing private-eye ninja is to protect the weak and the innocent.

There was nothing he could say to change my mind.

Well, almost nothing.

Me and Dante had to find Nasty Ned's hideout.

But where should we look first?

We checked the basement, but he wasn't there.

We checked Mr. Toots's closet.

He wasn't there either.

We actually couldn't figure out how to get onto the roof.

So we checked the gym.

The door was closed, so I did some spying. And guess what I heard.

It was the voice of Nasty Ned! And just like his picture, it sounded strangely familiar.

Go? Now? Leave it to Dante to chicken out just when we had the bad guy cornered.

We ran around the corner and watched the door. But it didn't open.

So we went back and looked inside.

The gym was empty. But the locker room door was wide open!

There were papers all over the floor. And in one corner, a big plastic box. It was filled with old clothes and hats and junk. Dante even found a tiny clue.

Luckily, I spotted an even bigger clue.

It was the biggest clue I'd ever seen. It didn't even look like a real phone! There could only be one explanation:

Whoever he was talking to must have been on the other end of that phone call. Suddenly, I had a brilliant idea: What if we pressed redial? Then we would find out who Nasty Ned was talking to!

I pressed the redial
button. But nothing
happened.

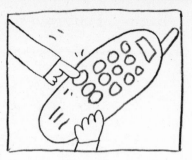

So I pressed it harder.
Still nothing.

I pressed it again. And again. And again.

I handed Dante the phone.

As usual, Dante
was making a huge
mistake!

I was just about to put the phone in my backpack
when the gym door opened. It was Coach Hugh!

He took the phone. Then he picked up the eye patch.

Suddenly I was really confused. What would
Coach Hugh want with an eye patch?

That's when Dante picked
up one of the papers on the
floor.

I took a look.

As you can see, there's a lot more to this mystery than I thought.

Love,
PJ

PS. I got your postcard, Dad! It was waiting for me when I got home from school!

YA-HOO!!

It sounds like things are awesome in Nashville! But now I'm really confused.

Why did you say the Secret Mission released their new recording of bad guys? Was it an accident? I thought it was supposed to be a secret. Now that you released it, won't everyone hear it?

Also, why is the Secret Mission going on tour? Are you looking for a new hideout? You can always hide out in my room if you want.

I just can't believe you're letting country music star Junior McFiddle ride in the same tour bus as you. I know you guys are friends now, but it still makes no sense. What happened? Did he quit music and become a private eye? Does he even have any cool skills?

If you needed a new partner, you should have asked me. I'm a way better private eye than him.

By the way, Chloe got the new autographed Junior McFiddle poster you sent. As usual, she acted like a big baby about it!

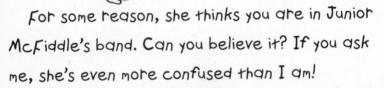

For some reason, she thinks you are in Junior McFiddle's band. Can you believe it? If you ask me, she's even more confused than I am!

I tried to tell her that she was wrong, but she wouldn't listen.

I tried not to tell her about the Secret Mission. But she was really getting on my nerves.

Finally, the truth just kind of slipped out.

Sorry about that, Dad. I know the Secret Mission is supposed to be our secret. But I couldn't help it. Luckily, I don't think she believed me anyway.

I guess some people can't see the truth even when it's right in front of their face.

Chapter Six

The Library Letter

SATURDAY, MAY 11

Dear Dad,

This morning, I tried to write Sara's new "Love
Pony" play. It would have been awesome if it
wasn't for one thing: I couldn't think of anything
to write.

Fortunately, I knew someone who did.

I guess Chloe doesn't know anything about ponies either.

As it turned out, writing a whole play by myself was harder than I thought. So I decided to take a break and spend the rest of the day playing Ninja Warz 3.

The cool thing about upgrading to Ninja Warz 3 is that I can play it on my game pad. That means I don't have to do any of the moves myself. It does everything for me!

It's not like the old days when I used to get in trouble for playing Ninja Warz 1 and 2.

The bad part is now Mom says I don't get enough exercise. But that's not exactly true either.

Mom keeps saying she wishes there was something more creative that I could do with my energy. Well, guess what? There is. It's called drumming! Ever since I got to play the drums in band, I can't stop thinking about how awesome it would be if I owned my own drum kit.

The only problem is drums cost a bazillion dollars. So I have to wait and find the perfect time to ask. But I'm sure it won't take long.

Meanwhile, I could hear Chloe watching Junior McFiddle's video for his new hit single, "Bad Guys."

I haven't bothered to watch it, but I guess his new band dresses up like a bunch of fake private eyes. It sounds pretty cheesy if you ask me.

An hour later, me and Chloe were still arguing. So Mom said it was time to turn off all the screens and go someplace peaceful where there was nothing to do but sit and read quietly.

Talk about weird. We never go to the library!

Before we left, I grabbed the newspaper with my famous picture in it. Just in case any librarians recognized me and wanted my autograph.

I also wore my Captain Big Boy cape so they could see what a hero I was.

Meanwhile, Mom took some posters for Chloe's ballet recital tomorrow. She said she wanted to hang them up on the community events board. She even let Chloe wear her horrible babyish ballet outfit. It was so embarrassing!

While we were in the car, Mom told us the real reason why she wanted to go to the library. She was looking for a book about country line dancing!

It didn't make any sense.

When we got to the library, Mom asked the librarian if they had a book about country line dancing.

That gave me an awesome idea!

The librarian made me walk all the way down to the end of this ridiculously long row of shelves. There were books everywhere! And they were huge!

She handed me a pony book. It was so big and heavy, I could barely hold it up.

The second one she gave me was even heavier!

After three books, my arms totally gave out.

I asked her why anyone would ever go to the library and read huge heavy books like these when they could just stay home and look stuff up online.

The librarian didn't answer.
She just went over and started
helping someone else.

I walked around the shelves to see who she was helping. It was Mr. Pastrami! What was he doing at the library? He doesn't read. He's a musician!

I didn't want him to see me with Chloe. So I hid behind the row of books. That's when I heard Mom talking to another librarian about Chloe's recital.

Chloe started doing her dance to "Love Pony." As usual, her moves were terrible. But the librarians started clapping anyway.

Only it wasn't real clapping. It was that quiet kind that adults do when they're trying to be polite. Talk about embarrassing! I had to act fast before Mr. Pastrami saw her!

At first I don't think they heard me, because no one got in line. So I showed them my picture in the newspaper.

One of the librarians took the paper from me.

I was shocked! Were they serious? Anyone?!

I sprang into action with some of the greatest
ninja break-dancing moves
I've ever done in my life.
Seriously, Dad. I was
incredible!

You could tell the librarians were ready to explode with applause!

But then Mr. Pastrami walked around the corner carrying a huge stack of CDs. As you can see, he wasn't even looking where he was going!

The next thing I knew, he crashed right into me!

Me, Mr. Pastrami, and all of the CDs went flying.

I just hope the librarians give him a warning
because I could have seriously gotten hurt.

Meanwhile, Mom made me pick up all of the CDs.
It wasn't even my fault! Here I was, peacefully
break-dancing in the library, when Mr. P. walked
right up and crashed into me! I mean, what was he
doing with all of those CDs anyway?

I must have picked up a hundred CDs. Most of them were boring old jazz CDs from a bazillion years ago. Only one of them had a "New" sticker on it.

There was something strangely familiar about it. So I studied it closely.

Can you believe it? Junior McFiddle named his new band "the Secret Mission"! He totally stole that name from your private-eye business! Isn't that illegal? I tried to stay calm, but it was impossible.

We have to stop him, Dad! Now everyone will find out about the Secret Mission. And it's all thanks to the library!

I told Mom we should arrest the librarians, but she just wanted to go home and watch her line-dancing video in peace and quiet.

Love,
PJ

PS. When we were leaving the library, we went by the community events board where the librarians hung Chloe's ballet poster. Only now there was a new poster there. When I saw it, I froze!

Not only was it a picture of Nasty Ned, but it said I could catch him at the Bunn Community Playhouse next Friday. That's the same theater where Chloe is doing her ballet recital tomorrow!

But who hung the poster up? And how do they know Nasty Ned will be at the Bunn?

One thing's for sure: Someone out there must really want me to catch him! But who?

As soon as we got home, Mom decided to go back to the library. She said there was something she forgot to take from the community events board. But I have no clue what it was.

This time, she made me wait in the car.

Chapter Seven

The Sweetchucks Letter

Dear Dad,

I stayed up all night thinking about how to catch Nasty Ned at the Bunn. I knew I would need a cool secret ninja weapon like a throwing star or nunchucks. But all I had in my backpack was a T-shirt, a bagel, and two stinky sweet dogs.

Suddenly, I had a brilliant idea: I could make my own weapon . . . with sweet dogs!

149

As soon as Mom left, I pulled both of them out of my backpack. They were harder and smellier than Coach Hugh's whistle! Using a piece of ribbon from Chloe's costume, I tied them together with slipknots.

As you can see, they made perfect nunchucks. You wouldn't believe how fast I could whip them around!

I just need a little practice tying slipknots.

I didn't want Mom to notice the big hole in the TV, so I covered it with my T-shirt.

Then I spent the rest of the morning looking up stuff about ponies on the Internet. It was funner than the library! And I learned some cool facts too!

For example, did you know that ponies have been alive since the days of the Wild West? Talk about old-fashioned! Back then, they didn't have video games OR hit singles. How boring! Seriously, Dad. What did those cowboys even do all day?

Not only that, did you know that some ponies learn to talk when they grow up? Don't believe me? Just check the Internet! I found tons of videos with real live talking horses!

Seriously, Dad. I don't know why we even need teachers or schools anymore. From now on, kids should just learn everything from the Internet.

Now that I've learned so many cool facts about ponies, writing this play will be a piece of cake!

Plus, look what else I found online:

HUGE SALES FOR HUGE GUYS!
TITO'S
BIG MAN'S SHOP

OLD-FASHIONED
TEN-GALLON HATS
(JUST LIKE JUNIOR McFIDDLE
    WEARS)
5% OFF WHILE SUPPLIES LAST

How lucky is that! As soon as I get one of those

s, I'll look like my picture in the paper again.

everyone will see that I'm really a famous

! But first, I have to beg Mom to take me.

Love,
PJ

PS. It worked! Mom said she would take me to

to's if I just promised

behave during Chloe's

llet recital this

ternoon. Who knew

ould be so easy!

NOW
WHERE DID
I PUT MY
SWEET-
CHUCKS?

Chapter Eight

The Recital Letter

Dear Dad,

When we got to Tito's, I went straight to the hat shelves and started trying on hats.

They had a lot of them, so it was hard to find the perfect one!

BUT SIR, ALL THESE HATS ARE EXACTLY THE SAME!

THAT'S WHAT *YOU* THINK!

Finally, on the top shelf, I found it! It looked exactly like my old ones! As usual, I forgot my money. Luckily, Mom had her credit card!

I offered to give the salesman my autograph too, but for some reason he only wanted Mom's.

I guess he didn't realize that my autograph is worth at least a bazillion hats. So I took out my newspaper.

I put the hat on to show him it was really me.

Anyone? Was he serious? It's a good thing I was wearing my break-dance suit under my clothes.

I was about to show him my break-dancing moves, but Mom said we were late for Chloe's recital. So we left.

We actually got to the recital early. But that was OK because it gave me a chance to show off my new hat. It worked too! People couldn't take their eyes off of me.

Mom wanted to sit in the front row to take close-up photos of the dancers. Meanwhile, I could tell the rest of the audience was really looking at me. And it was all thanks to my awesome hat!

Plus, you'll never guess who sat next to me! Give up? It was Officer Bill!

I was almost speechless!

Let me tell you, Dad, it was an incredible honor sitting next to a real local hero like Officer Bill. Now I know how other people must feel when they sit next to me!

Too bad the recital was so horrible. The dancing went on forever! You could tell everyone was getting restless and bored.

Chloe was the last one to dance. She put a tiny saddle on Teddy Snuffles so he looked like a pony. Then she started dancing around him in circles to "Love Pony." For some reason, she didn't even seem embarrassed!

♪ PONY!
PONY!
♫ PONY!
PONY!

Just then I spotted something suspicious. It was a shadowy figure lurking behind the curtain! I could only see his shape, but from where I was sitting, it looked exactly like Nasty Ned! Was it a trap? Was he here to steal my new hat? Or my star from Chloe's costume? There was only one thing for certain: I had to act fast!

Good thing I was wearing my ninja suit. I politely excused myself and started taking off my pants at the same time.

Except I didn't really go to the little boys' room. I went backstage to arrest Nasty Ned.

I took off my clothes and got out my sweetchucks. Then I looked around for Nasty Ned.

There he was! On the other side of the stage! I had to stop him before he got my star!

All of the ballerinas screamed and ran onto the stage! You could tell they were scared. They're just lucky I was there to protect them.

I whipped those chucks around as fast as I could!

Unfortunately,
my slipknot slipped . . .

SLIP!

and one of the chucks went
flying off into the audience.

OW!!

Then all of the ballerinas crashed into each other.

OW!

CRASH!

OW!

OW!

Meanwhile, Nasty Ned must have escaped through
the stage door. I couldn't find him anywhere.

Oh well. I didn't get my hat back, but at least he didn't steal my star. Once again, I saved the day!

By the way, I think my flying sweet dog might have hit Officer Bill, because when he climbed up onto the stage, he had a huge lump on his forehead.

Officer Bill told Mom that if anything like this ever happened again, he would take me down to the station. Can you believe it? What an honor!
Maybe he'll even give me a special hero award!

Even though Chloe's recital wasn't any good, you could tell Mom was really proud of me for saving her life. In fact, she was pretty much speechless the whole time we were leaving.

As we were driving away, I swore I saw Mr. Prince walking up the back steps to the theater carrying a bunch of brightly painted boxes.
I told Mom to turn the car around so we could warn him that Nasty Ned was on the loose. But for some reason, Mom wouldn't go back.

Love,
PJ

PS. When we got home, I decided to play Ninja Warz 2 to get ready for my next battle with Nasty Ned. After spending weeks staring at my game pad, it would have been nice to stare at a big screen for a change. There was only one problem:

Mom put her line-dancing video on. But she didn't get to watch it thanks to that huge hole in the TV.

After that, Mom tried to watch her video on the computer. But it didn't matter. The DVD was from the library, so it was all scratched up anyway.

DON'T CRY, MOMMY. I'LL TEACH YOU HOW TO DANCE.

Actually, that was good news, because I needed the computer to finish doing research for my play about ponies in the Wild West.

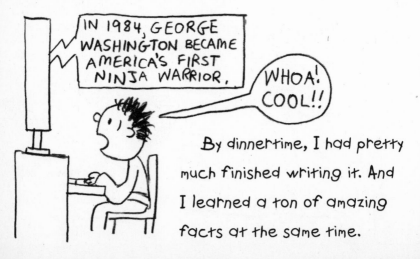

IN 1984, GEORGE WASHINGTON BECAME AMERICA'S FIRST NINJA WARRIOR.

WHOA! COOL!!

By dinnertime, I had pretty much finished writing it. And I learned a ton of amazing facts at the same time.

Not only that, I put them ALL in my play. I can't wait to show it to Coach Hugh tomorrow. He's going to love it!

As you can see, it was a pretty good day. I even had time before bed to copy Junior McFiddle's signature onto my new hat. Thanks to Chloe's new poster, it came out perfect!

Chapter Nine

The Second
Audition Letter

MONDAY, MAY 13

Dear Dad,

When I got to school this morning, I told Sara I
had pretty much finished writing the play.

I said it had everything she could want in a play.

She wanted to read it right then, but I told her she'd have to wait until the audition.

I couldn't stop thinking about it all morning. During silent reading, I got so excited, I almost read it out loud!

Seriously, Dad. It took all of my strength to wait.
So you can imagine how happy I was to see Coach
Hugh when he finally came to tell me it was time.

Sara was already waiting for me onstage.
I was surprised to see Mr. Prince there too.

Coach Hugh dimmed the lights. Then he yelled, "Action!" It was just like being in a real play!

There was a wild pony who looked a little bony. He said:

They called him Macaroni.

His owner made him tame.

George Washington was his name.

He was the world's first president. It brought him lots of fame!

He's on some dollar bills.

His shirt had lots of frills.

He chopped a cherry tree in half with awesome ninja skills!

The cherries were forgiving.

They grew where folks were living.

The Squantos had a picnic that they called the first Thanksgiving!

They held a dance contest.

The pony was the best!

He taught them all some break-dance moves, and then they moved out west.

The horse became a sleuth.

George grew a wooden tooth.

AND IF YOU GO ONLINE, THEN YOU WILL SEE THAT IT'S THE **TRUTH!**

Seriously, Dad. Was that incredible or what?!

You could tell Sara was amazed. She couldn't stop staring at me. Neither could Coach Hugh.

THANK YOU! THANK YOU!

Even Mr. Prince could barely speak. He looked at me. Then he looked at Coach Hugh. Then back at me.

Coach Hugh said it had everything you could ever want: action, adventure, ponies, AND JOKES!

For some reason, Sara didn't agree.

Mr. Prince told Sara to relax and calmly tell us what it was she didn't like about the play.

Mr. Prince wouldn't say who was right or wrong.
He just said me and Sara had to learn to discuss
our differences like professionals.

Later, at lunch, me and Sara did what Mr. Prince said. We discussed the play like professionals.

As you can see, Sara is impossible to work with. So it looked like the play was doomed.

Dante said he could try to fix the play for us. But I really didn't see how. Seriously, Dad! He's only in 3rd grade!

Dante told Sara he would rewrite the play so it was more like the hit single "Love Pony." But I still have a bad feeling about it.

Later, during outdoor recess, Sara wanted to take pictures for the play poster with her dad's camera.

Suddenly, I had a brilliant idea.

If I wore my new fake hat as a costume, it would be on posters everywhere. Then people would see me with a "real, signed" Junior McFiddle hat, and I would be famous again! I showed Sara my latest masterpiece.

That's when I saw Dante running across the playground.

Dante pulled something big, brown and hairy out of his backpack. It looked like a pony with all the air let out of it.

I couldn't believe it!

It was the coolest costume I've ever seen in my life! I think it's safe to say this pony suit is going to make me even more famous than the Junior McFiddle hat.

There was just one problem.

The Taylor Girls would not quit bugging us.

Dante tried to take pictures of me and Sara in our costumes, but the Taylor Girls ruined everything!

We had to find someone who could help us. Someone who knew more about taking pictures than Dante.

Luckily, I had a brilliant idea.

We went inside to the art room. It was completely dark. Ms. Julian was nowhere to be found.

Even worse, someone had taken the sheet off my secret weapon. It was just sitting there. Naked! Now everyone could see what I was making!

Dante said I should make my art smaller before it fell on someone and flattened them.

I looked around for the sheet, but it was missing. So were all of Ms. Julian's papier-mâché gallons of ice cream.

I think it was clear what had happened. Nasty Ned had stolen everything!

Everything except the sheet.

Dante dove on top of me just as my secret weapon crashed down behind us.

Luckily, the chair got in the way. Otherwise, I would have been flattened!

Sara said Dante saved my life. But that's not
true. We both know it was really saved by the chair.

I picked up the sheet again, and my art project fell
off the table.

There was a long red string tied between the
sheet and my art. That's why it fell on me.

It was Nasty Ned! All I can say is, he better watch out. Once I finish building my secret weapon, he'll wish he never messed with PJ McGee.

Love,
PJ

PS. I also had gym today. We were playing dodgeball, which is not exactly my favorite sport.

For some reason, Coach Hugh told me I couldn't wear my pony suit during dodgeball anymore. He probably thought it gave me an unfair advantage. So I had to put it back in his costume box.

Except when I looked in the box, you'll never guess what I saw! Right on top was a long red piece of string! It was the same kind that Nasty Ned used to set the trap for me. Don't ask me how it got in Coach Hugh's costume box, though.

Unfortunately, Sara had already given the camera back to her dad. Leave it to her to mess everything up!

As you can see, I'm going to have to start looking out for myself from now on.

Chapter Ten

The Clam Letter

TUESDAY, MAY 14

Dear Dad,

The dance party is only two days away. As you can guess, I've been working like crazy on both my ninja moves and my break-dancing moves. By now, I'm so awesome at both, a lot of people can't tell the difference!

Me and Dante had Ninja Club again today.
Mr. Prince was going to teach us how to do a
slide kick. But I've already mastered that move.

So while he taught Dante, I searched the gym
for booby traps. I started by looking in Mr. Prince's
duffel bag.

I didn't find any traps in there, but I did find
something strange.

Don't ask me why
Mr. Prince would
keep a fake beard
in his gym bag.

I was about to put it back when Mr. Toots
saw me.

Meanwhile, Dante was still trying to do his
slide kick.

Mr. Prince took one step back and slipped on the beard.

Luckily, I sprang into action.

All I can say is, it's a good thing I was there to catch him. He could have gotten seriously hurt on that thing.

Too bad Mr. Toots wasn't so lucky. He also slipped on the beard.

Then he crashed into Mr. Prince.

Meanwhile, Dante added the slide to his kick. He slid right under both of them!

Luckily, he only kicked a dodge ball.

The ball went flying safely the other way.

Then it bounced off of Coach Hugh's costume box.

And flew back toward them.

It just missed.

And hit Mr. Toots's bucket instead.

After they got soaked, I had a feeling Mr. Prince was done teaching us ninja moves for the day.

In the end, Mr. Prince told me he was thinking of canceling Ninja Club forever. But that's OK. I already know all of his moves anyway.

I was about to go to class when Dante handed me something.

Dante said he rewrote it to be more like Junior McFiddle's hit single. As you know, "Love Pony" is all about love and hugging. So I was afraid there would be tons of horrible stuff like that in it.

I nervously read it during silent reading.

It was short. But, believe it or not, it wasn't terrible.

Then I read act two.

I couldn't believe it! A hugging scene? Was he crazy? I tried to stay calm, but it wasn't easy.

Mrs. Sikes said if I had a problem, I should discuss it with Mr. Prince in the principal's office.

Unfortunately, Mr. Prince didn't think so.

IF YOU HAVE A PROBLEM WITH THIS, YOU SHOULD DISCUSS IT WITH DANTE.

BUT THAT'S A TERRIBLE IDEA!!

DANCE PARTY NEXT THURSDAY FUN FRIDAY

I turned to leave just as Coach Hugh walked in wearing an eye patch and carrying a jump rope. We would have crashed as usual, only this time I was ready with an incredible slide kick!

HI-YAH!

Suddenly, I froze. That rope! That eye patch! I had seen them before. But where?

I'D STAY AND CHAT, BUT I'M A LITTLE TIED UP RIGHT NOW.

OH... YEAH... TIED UP. I GET IT.

Mr. Prince said that he and Coach Hugh needed to have a private meeting. So I decided to wait outside and do a little spying. And here's what I heard:

Suddenly, it all made sense! The rope! The eye patch! The red strings! Coach Hugh was Nasty Ned in disguise! He's the one who stole my hats!

I had to tell someone fast. So I screamed for help. But, as usual, there wasn't anyone helpful around.

So I told Dante.

I thought Dante would freak out. But he didn't.

If you ask me, Dante wasn't taking this problem very seriously.

When we got to lunch, Mrs. Browny was serving her famous clam chowder. As you know, she puts the world's chewiest clams in there. It can take hours just to chew one.

Meanwhile, I practically begged Dante to take the hugging scene out of the play.

That's when Sara showed up holding my pony costume.

I wasn't sure which was worse: doing a play with Nasty Ned, or a hugging scene with Sara.

Plus, it was still lunchtime. So pretty much the whole school was going to see me and Sara hug onstage!

By the time Coach Hugh arrived, me and Sara and Dante were already onstage.

OK, BIG GUY, SPIT OUT THE GUM BEFORE YOU CHOKE ON IT!

IT'S A CLAM!

CHEW CHEW

HE DOESN'T LOOK LIKE NASTY NED TO ME.

YEAH! I THOUGHT NED HAD AN EYE PATCH!

Coach Hugh yelled, "Action!" and we all started acting. Amazingly, we got through the entire first act without any mistakes.

I AM A GIRL!

I AM A PONY!

AND I AM GEORGE WASHINGTON!

Then it was time for act two: the love scene! The Taylor Girls were sitting right in the front row just waiting for me and Sara to hug!

My heart was beating like crazy!

My pony suit was incredibly hot.
I started to sweat.

I felt a lump in my throat!
I could barely breathe!

Then ...

ACK!
ACK!
ACK!

UM...
I THINK
PJ LOST
HIS
VOICE
AGAIN.

Suddenly, I realized I wasn't acting. I really couldn't breathe! I was choking on Mrs. Browny's clam!

Sara ran around behind me!

She wrapped her arms around me and squeezed!

Except it wasn't a hug! It was the move that Officer Bill taught us!

The next thing I knew, the clam popped out!

It flew all the way across the stage and landed right in Taylor Z.'s mouth!

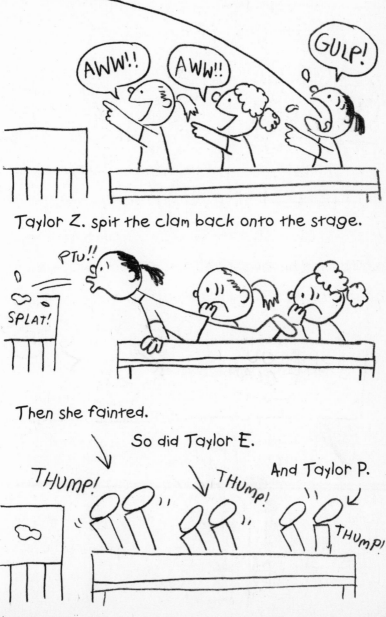

Taylor Z. spit the clam back onto the stage.

Then she fainted.

So did Taylor E.

And Taylor P.

Suddenly, the whole cafeteria burst into applause. You could tell everyone thought I was a hero!

THANK YOU! THANK YOU!

Everyone except for Dante.

SARA SAVED PJ'S LIFE! SHE'S A HERO!

Can you believe it? All she did was give me a couple squeezes. I'd hardly call that being a hero.

Meanwhile, the three of us went to the nurse. Sara's dad was there too.

I'M SO PROUD OF MY LITTLE HERO!

THANKS DAD.

HA!

I think it's safe to say, if you were here, you would have said the same thing about me!

While the nurse called Mom, Coach Hugh stopped by. This time, he was wearing the eye patch!

Suddenly I remembered: My hat! Sara dropped it on the stage! Before anyone could stop me, I raced back to the cafeteria.

But I was too late. It was already gone! Only the clam remained.

I was about to pick it up when Mr. Toots stepped out from behind the curtain.

It was the last straw. I just couldn't take it anymore!

As you can see, this whole day turned out horrible: Hugging! Choking! Hat stealing! And if that's not bad enough, my favorite gym teacher turned out to be the thief!

By the time I got back to the nurse's office, everyone else had gone back to class. There was nothing to do but sit and wait for Mom.

It took forever! By the time she got there,
even the nurse had gone.

As you know, Mom can be kind of embarrassing
in these situations.

So I'm kind
of glad it was
just me and her.

Love,
PJ

Chapter Eleven

The Hero Letter

WEDNESDAY, MAY 15

Dear Dad,

Ever since Sara gave me the Heimlich maneuver, everyone has been calling her a local hero. Especially Mr. Prince! He even invited a world-famous guest to give her an award.

Officer Bill walked onstage with his horse puppet in one hand and some kind of fake-looking medal in the other.

TELL ME, SNOWBALL, WHICH IS THE HAIRIEST SIDE OF A HORSE?

I DON'T KNOW, OFFICER BILL. WHICH?

THE OUTSIDE!

No one laughed.

BUT SERIOUSLY, KIDS, DON'T BE A ZERO. GIVE IT UP FOR A REAL LOCAL HERO: MISS CLARA BELLUM!

He gave Sara the medal, and everyone started cheering! Can you believe it? Sara got all of the fame, but I was the one who did all the choking. It just wasn't fair!

Officer Bill even said he would do a special break-dance in Sara's honor.

He was about to do a one-armed Safety Grinder, but then he slipped on something.

It was my clam!

I guess Mr. Toots forgot to pick it up after he yelled at me yesterday.

Officer Bill crashed into the flagpole.

The flagpole crashed into the curtain,

and the curtain crashed down onto the stage.

After Sara got her medal, people instantly started treating her like she was famous.

Dante even made a
poster of her wearing
MY Junior McFiddle hat!
He just cut out all the
parts with the Taylor Girls.

The next time I saw
Sara was during lunch.
She was surrounded by
a huge group of kids and acting like a total snob.

If you ask me, I liked her better when no one
liked her.

To tell you the truth, even Dante was starting to bug me. Ever since Sara became friends with us, it's been hard to tell whose side he's really on.

Dante said it was cool having a famous friend like Sara.

Suddenly the whole cafeteria started chanting Sara's name. A bunch of kids lifted her up and carried her around the room.

One of them kicked my chair as they went by.

I couldn't take it anymore. I had to make them stop. That's when I spotted Mr. Prince's megaphone on the stage. He must have left it there when he went to the nurse with Officer Bill. I leapt up and grabbed it!

I told everyone they must be crazy to cheer for Sara. Couldn't they see what total idiots they looked like?

The room went silent. They were all stunned. It was a dirty job, but someone had to tell them the truth!

Everyone gasped!

As Mrs. Sikes walked me to the principal's office, the crowd just stood there staring. It was pretty clear who was famous now: ME!

When I got to Mr. Prince's office, he didn't look too happy to see me.

For some reason, that only made him madder.

He said I should be standing up for my friends.

Not calling them names just to get attention.

Mr. Prince shook his head.

Mr. Prince sat down. All of a sudden, he looked really tired.

There was only one way I was going to get my hats back from Coach Hugh: I had to defeat him in battle! But how? He was huge!

Even if I used all my ninja moves at once, it would still be like battling a bazillion bad guys.

I needed a partner: A real hero who could back me up while I defeated him.

Then I remembered something Mr. Prince said about kindness and helping others. So I decided to help Sara.

I wasn't sure why she was still mad at me, but I think it had something to do with a nasty rumor the Taylor Girls were spreading around school.

So I thought of another way to help!

I even knew the perfect way to do it: with a poster! Luckily, I could just write on top of Dante's poster. That way I didn't actually have to draw a picture of Sara.

It was probably the kindest thing I've ever done. And the best part: it was easy! The whole thing only took me a couple seconds!

But believe it or not, it didn't work.

Sara was still mad.

So was Dante.

So I guess it was up to me to battle Coach Hugh all by myself.

I went straight to the gym. I have to admit, I was still a little nervous. But only because I wasn't wearing my ninja suit.

He was in there, all right! I had him right where I wanted him.

I was about to kick down the door when I felt a tap on my shoulder.

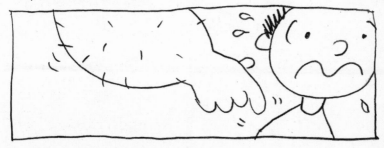

I slowly turned around.

It was Coach Hugh!

It didn't make any sense! I had just heard his voice coming from the gym. How could he be in two places at once?

Normally, I would have battled him right then. But the timing wasn't right. I had lost the element of surprise! Now there was only one thing left to do.

It was actually a good thing I ran.
As you can see, I barely made it
back to Mrs. Sikes's room alive!

After school, I went back to the gym for a
rematch, but Coach Hugh was gone. I guess he got
scared, because all I found was a note on the door:

FOUL PLAY?! That meant Coach Hugh was planning to do something terrible! But what? And where? And when? My only hope was to finish building my secret weapon before he struck again.

As I turned to leave, I spotted a tiny piece of paper on the ground right below the note.

I thought it might be a clue, but it was only a tiny letter "a."

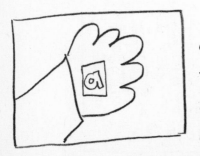

Don't ask me where it came from. It probably fell out of some magazine. As you can see, it was no help at all.

When I got to the art room, it was full of all the papier-mâché decorations the Taylor Girls made:

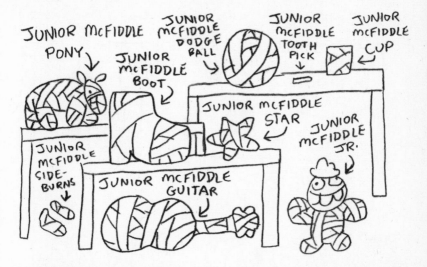

My secret weapon was the only original thing there.

It took me all afternoon, but I finally finished it! Now, I just hope the paint dries in time for the official McFiddle Day dance party tomorrow.

Meanwhile, Taylor Z. was working on her decoration too.

As you can see, this was going to be the all-time worst-decorated dance party ever.

Love,
PJ

PS. When I got home, Mom said she had good news. At first, I thought I was about to become famous again.

It was pretty much the worst news ever.

Seriously, Dad. I can't go to a dance with my mom. She embarrasses me everyplace we go. I honestly couldn't imagine anything worse.

Why would she talk to Coach Hugh? Didn't she
realize how dangerous he is?

Not only that, how did she get his phone number?

As I was searching for a clue,
I accidentally bumped into Mom's
purse and something fell out.

It was an ad.

I saw the same sign
on the events board
at the library! Mom
must have taken it
and called the number.

As you can see, she was in **HUGE** trouble!

Chapter Twelve

The Dance Party Letter

THURSDAY, MAY 16

Dear Dad,

Today was the dance party. I wore my ninja suit under my clothes so this time I would be ready to battle Coach Hugh. I just hoped nothing embarrassing would happen.

Now that my secret weapon was finished, I was ready for anything. So as soon as I got to school, I looked around for Coach Hugh.

I checked the gym.

I checked the nurse's office.

I even checked Mr. Toots's closet.

But I couldn't find him anywhere.

When it was time for the dance party, the Taylor Girls brought their decorations to the cafeteria. They had painted hearts on all of them.

Meanwhile, I needed a little help with mine because it was so awesomely huge.

Under the sheet, the paint was almost dry. But I brought an extra can just in case.

We had just finished setting up the decorations when Mr. Prince arrived with a special guest.

Mr. Pastrami picked up his tuba and played "Love Pony." Everyone started dancing. Well, almost everyone. A few people were still missing.

The real mystery was why Coach Hugh wasn't there. Then, all of a sudden,

He was there! And he was wearing a ten-gallon hat!

I tried to grab it, but he wouldn't stop dancing!

That's when Dante called my name. He was holding the note I found yesterday on the gym door. You know, the one that said "get ready for foul play"? Well, it turned out, that tiny letter "a" had fallen off the note! Dante said it changed everything.

They were line dancing together!

I had to stop them! Mom was in serious danger! Plus, she was a horrible dancer!

I took off all my clothes and showed Coach Hugh my ninja suit.

But he wouldn't give it back. He said the hat belonged to him!

I was about to use it in a surprise attack.

I couldn't lift it. It was too big!

I tried again from the other side.

I almost had it!

But it was too heavy! My grip was slipping!

RRR!!!

It was going to crush me!

That's when I heard the scream.

NOOoo!!!!

It was Dante!

He flew across the stage and did an amazing slide kick! I thought he was going to use it on Coach Hugh. But he didn't.

He used it on me!

We both fell backward. My secret weapon went flying out of my hands. It would have flattened us, but the hat table saved our lives.

Meanwhile, Sara started yelling and pointing at Taylor E.'s hat. My secret weapon had chopped right through the papier-mâché.

Leave it to Sara to be totally obvious.

I picked up the hat and started peeling away the outside layer. Believe it or not, she was right. Under the papier-mâché was my Junior McFiddle hat!

243

It even had the signature!

Suddenly, Dante jumped up and karate-chopped the other two papier-mâché hats.

It looked like Coach Hugh didn't steal my hats after all. One of the Taylor Girls did. But which one?

As you can see, it was impossible to tell who really did it!

I had to admit, even I was a little confused. If Coach Hugh didn't do it, then where did he get HIS hat?

That was because they had just set the trap.

Believe it or not, it actually kind of made

sense. Except for one thing:

Dante said all of those clues were really just costumes and props for his play. And all of the times I heard them talk about ten gallons, they were actually just practicing their lines. That's why they kept saying the same thing over and over.

Just then, Mr. Prince made an announcement.

Ok. Fine. So it really was a play.

But that was impossible! In all the posters, Nasty Ned didn't have a mustache. And Mr. Prince does!

That explained why I saw both Mr. Prince and Nasty Ned at the Bunn during Chloe's ballet recital. They were actually the same person!

I know it all sounds incredible, but it looked like Dante was right about everything.

Once again, I had solved the mystery. Thanks to me, Coach Hugh was innocent, and everyone was safe.

Even better, I got my hats back! All three of them! There was only one problem:

They looked exactly the same. My signatures were so incredible, it was impossible to tell them apart!

I looked at Dante.

Then I looked at
one of the hats.

I looked at Sara.

Then I looked at
another hat.

Suddenly, I knew what I had to do:

I had to wear all three hats at once. That way
I'd be three times as famous as I was before!

Pretty much everyone thought it was a brilliant idea.

But believe it or not, my next idea was even brillianter:

After that, I only had one hat left. But for some reason, I still felt like a hero. A REAL hero!

Sara and Dante seemed to like their new hats. As soon as they put them on, kids started asking them for autographs.

It was weird, but no one even asked me for my autograph. Only this time, I didn't care. As you know, there's more to life than being famous.

Love,

PJ

PS. For some reason, after Mr. Prince saw me give my hats to Sara and Dante, he started acting really nice to me.

He said he had given it some thought, and decided to let me have a break-dancing contest after all.

Believe it or not, I could only find one person brave enough to challenge me.

The next thing I knew, Officer Bill was doing an incredible back spin. He was faster than ever, and he didn't even need to use his arms!

Then I jumped in and did the worm. Everyone was cheering for me. Even Chloe.

I don't know who was better. All I can say is, the crowd was screaming my name the whole time!

Luckily, I just missed slipping in a puddle of paint. Talk about a serious safety hazard! I'm not sure how it got there, but Officer Bill was about to slip in it too!

I sprang into action. As usual, I barely had time to think about what I was doing!

Did I use ninja moves?

Or break-dancing moves?

Or something totally original?

I really couldn't tell.

All I know is when Officer Bill needed a hero,

I was right there
saving his life!

Later, when Officer Bill got back from the nurse,
he gave me a high five. I only wish he hadn't lost
his voice, because I'm pretty sure he would have
called me a hero. Luckily, Ms. Julian took a photo of
us together. So now I have proof.

Chapter Thirteen

The Play Letter

Dear Dad,

Your package arrived today. I have to say, I was really excited when I saw it in the mail. It was the exact same size and shape as a new video game.

I tore off the paper as fast as I could.

Let's just say it wasn't what I expected.

Even though Chloe already downloaded all of the songs for free on the Internet, it's still cool to have the little booklet, I guess. To be honest, I've been so busy, I haven't actually looked at it yet. But I will.

By the way, Mom officially signed up to take country line dancing lessons from Coach Hugh. She may not be a good dancer, but she seems happy doing it. So I guess you could say that's pretty awesome.

At school today, I heard that the Taylor Girls got three detentions each! Even better, they're not allowed to call themselves the Taylor Girls anymore. I think it's safe to say they've learned their lesson.

Also, in band, Mr. Pastrami let me play the school's new drum kit. I guess he must really think I'm getting good. And you know what? I agree.

He told me I should also think about apologizing to Coach Hugh for calling him a hat thief. Well, I thought about it, and I decided to do something even more helpful than apologize.

I decided to help him make posters for his play!

As you can see, it's pretty much the best poster I ever made. Plus, I even autographed it for him!

For free!

When he saw it, he was so happy, he could barely speak.

By the way, for lunch today, Mrs. Browny was serving cheesy sweet dogs with clam sauce. And this time, they were fresh!

When I saw Sara and Dante in the cafeteria, I couldn't believe my eyes. They were holding hands!

He said they had just started a new private-eye business together. Can you believe it?! Sara and Dante? Private eyes?

Sara said if I really wanted to join their business, we all had to be equal partners.

On second thought, maybe equal wasn't such a bad idea.

Everyone secretly knows I'm the leader anyway.

Love,

PJ

PS. Tonight, Mr. Bellum took me and Sara and Dante to see Coach Hugh's play at the Bunn Community Playhouse. Luckily, we got front-row seats. As usual, people stared at us the whole time. I guess they could tell we were all famous heroes.

As the play began, a lot of things finally started to make sense. For example, you could tell Coach Hugh had made the program because it was written with little cut-up letters.

Also, Mr. Pastrami performed all of the music for the play on his muted tuba.

On the stage, Nasty Ned's hideout was filled with lots of brightly painted papier-mâché containers.

As it turned out, Ned wasn't stealing ten-gallon hats. He was stealing ice cream! Ten gallons of it!

Finally, when Mr. Prince came out onstage, I could barely recognize him.

He was wearing the fake eye patch and the fake beard. He was even talking on the giant fake phone.

For some reason, a couple people laughed.

Then Coach Hugh came out carrying a flashlight. He was playing a private eye, but he seemed kind of clueless.

Suddenly, the whole audience burst out laughing. I was shocked! Talk about rude!

But they wouldn't stop. No matter how much I yelled at them, they just kept laughing.

For the last scene, Nasty Ned and the private eye climbed off the stage and performed down on the floor! Now it felt like we were all part of the play!

Then Nasty Ned slipped on something!

It was my long-lost sweet dog! The same one that smacked Officer Bill during Chloe's recital.

It had been right there in the Bunn the whole time!

Nasty Ned hit the ground and just lay there.
That's when I noticed I was the only one laughing.
The crowd was silent.
Was this an accident?
Was he really out cold?
I had to find out!

Then . . .
slowly . . .
he smiled.

It was all part of the act. Coach Hugh had planned the whole thing.

I was acting in a real play, and I didn't even know it!

Everyone jumped up and started cheering as Coach Hugh and Mr. Prince climbed onto the stage to take their bows.

Since I was now part of the play, I decided to take my bow too. In a way, you could say I was the most realistic actor on the stage.

Seriously, Dad. If I keep this up, I could probably become the most famous actor who ever lived.

Chapter Fourteen

The CD Letter

SATURDAY, MAY 18

Dear Dad,

After the play last night, the Bunn guys handed out free posters. They were perfect for autographing!

Even though the line went all the way around the block, I told fans it would be worth the wait.

Because, one at a time, Mr. Prince and Coach Hugh signed them all.

How awesome is that!

Not only did I get autographs from world-famous actors, but they're both REAL friends of mine!

When I got home, I hung the poster up next to my bed. I think you'll agree, it's way cooler than anything signed by Junior McFiddle.

Believe it or not, I told Chloe she could borrow my hat. I'm sure she'll totally ruin it. But she looked so happy when I said yes, I almost didn't care.

It was a little too small for me anyway.

Love,
PJ

PS. I was just about to fall asleep when I saw the CD you sent me sitting next to my bed.

Don't ask me why, but for some reason, every

time I was about to open the little booklet, I got nervous and couldn't look at it.

Then, tonight, I looked.

The first thing I saw was this close-up picture of Junior McFiddle with his band playing behind him.

Then I looked closer. And my incredible eye for detail spotted something else:

It was a picture of you! Playing the drums! In his band!

At first, I wasn't sure if it was a joke. I guess I was just so surprised. And confused. I have to admit, I never expected it.

But I gave it some thought.

And now it makes total sense.

Pretending to play the drums in Junior McFiddle's band is pretty much the best disguise a private eye could ever have! I just have one question:

Now that the Secret Mission is working undercover with Junior McFiddle, can I still come out to Nashville and fight bad guys with you?

Don't worry, Dad. Your secret will be safe with me.

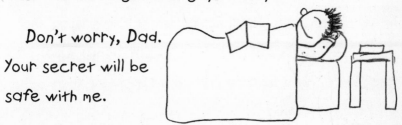

Acknowledgments

JEFF ↓

Hi, everyone! This is the page where Jeff Mack said I'm supposed to thank all the people who helped me become a rich and famous author. So, in case you want their autographs too, here they are: my editor, Mr. Green, his assistant, Mr. Geffen, my art director, Ms. Megged, my agent, Mr. Pfeffer, Jeff's friends, Ms. Paluck and Dillon, and Jeff's mom and dad. Thank you! Thank you! You are all awesome!

Jeff also wants me to thank his 4th-grade teacher, Mrs. Simiele, for liking the weird poems he wrote in her class. Or at least for saying she did. If it wasn't for her and lots of other cool teachers, he wouldn't still be writing his own stuff. So thanks!

Chapter One

THE
END.